CLASS PETS

Survival School

FRANK ASCH

Illustrated by John Kanzler

SIMON & SCHUSTER BOOKS FOR YOUNG READERS

NEW YORK LONDON TORONTO SYDNEY SINGAPORE

SIMON & SCHUSTER BOOKS FOR YOUNG READERS
An imprint of Simon & Schuster Children's Publishing Division
1230 Avenue of the Americas, New York, New York 10020
Text copyright © 2003 by Frank Asch
Illustrations copyright © 2003 by John Kanzler
All rights reserved, including the right of reproduction in whole or in
part in any form.
SIMON & SCHUSTER BOOKS FOR YOUNG READERS is a trademark of
Simon & Schuster, Inc.
Book design by O'Lanso Gabbidon
The text for this book is set in Trump Mediaeval.
The illustrations for this book are rendered in pencil.
Manufactured in the United States of America
2 4 6 8 10 9 7 5 3 1
CIP data for this book is available from the Library of Congress
ISBN 0-689-84657-6

FIRST
EDITION

To Emily and Ava and their class pet, Taffy—F. A.

For Theo—J. K.

Chapter 1

Wake up!" Molly leaned over Jake's nest and nudged him with her nose. "The new class pet just escaped!"

"What are you talking about?" Jake groaned and pulled some blue yarn over his face. "There's no new class pet!"

"Oh yes, there is!" insisted Molly. "Miss Clark bought him at Pretty Pets on her lunch break and already he's on the loose."

"On the loose?" Jake sat up and rubbed the sleep from his eyes.

"The kids are chasing him around the classroom and Miss Clark can't get them back in their seats!" said Molly.

"This I've got to see!" Jake yawned, rolled out of his nest, and shuffled over to the peephole.

The peephole was a tiny hole in the wall near Molly's nest. Through it Jake saw a classroom in total chaos. Kids were running around opening drawers and closet doors or on their hands and knees waving rulers and yardsticks under bookcases and cabinets. Some mischief makers had even started a game of tag, and two boys in the back of the room were having a punching match.

Miss Clark rarely raised her voice to discipline her students, but today she was shouting, "Everyone! Back into your seats! Right now!"

Then Marvin Towner opened the door to the art materials closet, and a dark yellow streak lit out across the classroom floor.

"There he is! Over there!" cried Marvin, and a crowd of kids surged after the furry fugitive, a gerbil the class had just named Dexter.

"Don't let Dexter get away!" They called to one another. "Over there! Over there!"

"I got him!" cried a blond-haired boy as he dove to the floor. But the jumpy gerbil slipped out of his hands and ducked behind Miss Clark's bookcase.

Seizing the opportunity to gain control of her classroom, Miss Clark ran to the bookcase and spun around to face her students.

"Everyone in your seats *now*!" she demanded.

Miss Clark, usually neat and composed, looked like someone caught up in a soccer riot. Her long black hair was messed, part of her blouse had come untucked, and her cheeks were flushed bright red.

With hands planted firmly on her hips, Miss Clark's eyes moved from student to student. Stopped in their tracks by her stony stare, the shouting, shoving, pushing, and punching stopped. Then slowly but surely, without Miss Clark having to say another word, everyone returned to their seats.

Breathing a sigh of relief, Miss Clark straightened her hair and tucked in her blouse. Then she calmly and politely asked two students, Rachel and Jason, to position themselves at either end of the bookcase.

"Get ready," she instructed them. "When I pull the bookcase away from the wall, don't let Dexter get past you."

"Don't worry, I'll catch him," said Jason.

"And please be gentle with our new class pet," cautioned Miss Clark. "He's one very frightened ger- bil right now, and we don't want to make things any worse for him."

"We'll be careful," replied Jason. Rachel nodded.

Miss Clark took a deep breath, grabbed hold of the bookcase with both hands, and slowly inched it away from the wall.

Rachel and Jason strained to see into the dark space behind the bookcase. But all they saw were some dust balls, a marble, and a few paper clips. Even when the bookcase was a good twelve inches away from the wall, there was no sign of Dexter.

"That's weird," said Jason as he picked up the marble and put it in his pocket. "It's like he disap- peared into thin air."

"Maybe we should have called him Houdini!" said Rachel.

It was then that Miss Clark noticed the molding behind the bookcase was loose. She pushed the book- case completely aside, got down on her knees, and poked her fingers behind the molding into empty space.

"Oh, my!" she gasped as the bell rang to announce the end of the school day, "It looks like Dexter escaped into the wall!"

Chapter 2

When Jake and Molly met Dexter inside the walls of P.S. 42, they could just barely make out the sheen of his yellowish brown fur, the white hairs on his cheeks, and his dark intense eyes. But there was no mistaking the fear in his voice.

"Who are you?" he demanded as soon as he smelled their approach. "If you want to fight, I'm ready! But watch out. I'm fierce and mean. The last foe I fought *never* stopped bleeding!"

Oh, give me a break, thought Jake. *I know fierce and mean. And you're about as fierce and mean as a candy cane!* But Jake kept these thoughts to himself and let Molly do the talking.

"Take it easy," she said calmly. "We're friends. My name is Molly. And this is my brother, Jake. We just came by to say hello."

Hearing the warmth and friendliness in Molly's voice, Dexter immediately relaxed.

"Hi," he said. "I guess my name is Dexter."

"You *guess*?" asked Jake.

"Well, that's the name Miss Clark and her kids gave me," replied Dexter. "They voted on it. There were lots of other names, like Fluffy and Hotdog and Pooky, but Dexter's the name that won."

"What about the name your momma gave you?" asked Molly.

There was an awkward pause. Then Dexter sighed and said, "Lots of my brothers and sisters got names. But Mom got sold before she got around to naming me."

"Well, I think Dexter is a nice name," said Molly as she wet her paws and washed her small round ears and pretty face. "A very nice name. Much better than Hot Dog or Pooky."

"Yeah, you're lucky," agreed Jake. "The kids in Mr. Applebaum's class call their guinea pig 'Blooper.'"

"You bet I'm lucky!" said Dexter. "First day and I'm already out of my cage. When did you two escape?"

"Escape?" chuckled Jake. "You got us all wrong, pal. We never escaped. We're house mice."

"That's right," said Molly. "But we never lived in a house. Before P.S. 42 we lived in a deli. So you might call us 'school mice.'"

"Or deli mice," added Jake.

"House mouse, school mouse, deli mouse?" Dexter scratched his chin. "What kind of pets are those?"

"Pets!" squeaked Jake as if he were insulted. "We were *never* pets. We take care of ourselves."

"That's what I want to do." said Dexter. "Only . . ." Dexter sighed and looked wistful. "I'm not sure I know how. Is it difficult to find food out here?"

"Naaaah," said Jake. "You'd be amazed at the tasty grub kids leave in their desks. Just last week I found half a cheese sandwich in someone's pencil case."

"I didn't like the mustard but the cheese lasted for days," said Molly.

At the mention of the word *cheese*, Dexter's eyes widened.

"I heard about cheese," he said. "A puppy at Pretty Pets told me all about it. Never had any myself, though."

"Never had any cheese!" exclaimed Molly. "Why you poor, poor thing! That's like a rabbit who never had a carrot, or a horse who never tasted hay."

"Or a cat who never ate a mouse," said Jake.

Dexter sighed and said, "In my entire lifetime I've only eaten one thing; gerbil food."

"What's gerbil food?" asked Jake.

"Mostly seeds and some green pellets made with . . . I don't know what . . . and vitamins," replied Dexter.

"Doesn't sound so bad," said Jake noticing that he was very much in the mood for a snack. "I *like* seeds."

"Gerbil food doesn't *taste* bad," replied Dexter. "But how would you like to eat the same thing day after day, week after week, *month* after *month*?"

"Our poppa would say that's 'too much of a good thing,'" replied Molly.

"Personally, I'd end up chewing on my toes," added Jake.

"They may have given you nothing but gerbil food at Pretty Pets, but you'll get plenty of treats here," said Molly.

"Oh, really," said Dexter. "Like what?"

"Miss Clark will give you carrots, lettuce,

peanuts, things like that," answered Molly. "And the kids will slip you sweets from time to time. They're told not to, but they do it anyway."

"There was nothing *sweet* about the kid who nearly squeezed me to death. I thought my belly button was going to pop!" complained Dexter. "And the kid who dropped me on my head wasn't so wonderful either. That's when I decided to take off."

"I saw what happened from our peephole," said Molly. "Good thing it was Stanley. He's kind of short."

"Yeah, well it still hurt!" Dexter rubbed the bump between his ears with both paws.

"I don't think anyone should have to live in a cage if they don't want to," said Jake. "But that bump is nothing compared to what could happen to you out here."

"Jake's right," said Molly. "If you ask me, the smartest thing you could do is turn around and go back to your cage right now. You may not think so now, but class pets are the luckiest animals in the world! I know, because Miss Clark's other class pets, Peaches the rabbit, Prince and Princess the lovebirds, and Gino the hamster, are my *best* friends."

"Hamster?" said Dexter. "I didn't see any hamster in the classroom."

"That's because Gino's a ghost," said Jake. "He liked being a class pet so much, when he died he came back for more."

"He's at a Dead Pet Society meeting this week," said Molly. "But if you stick around, I'm sure he'll tell you how wonderful it is to be a class pet."

"Thanks for the advice," said Dexter. "But growing up in a cage was bad enough. I don't want to die in one. What I really need is some advice on how to survive out here on my own."

Suddenly Molly pictured herself as a mouse-sized version of her idol, Miss Clark, teaching a class of one.

"You're making a *big* mistake . . ." she said, tugging thoughtfully on her long, even whiskers. "But Jake and I would be glad to teach you a few things."

At that moment Jake was busy thinking about gerbil food. So when Molly turned to him and said, "Wouldn't we Jake?"

He just replied, "Huh?"

Chapter 3

"urvival school is now in session!" declared Molly as she led the way past a loose brick onto the basement floor.

"Whatever you say, Teach," said Dexter. "What's my first lesson?"

"Water," said Molly. "I know Miss Clark said your folks come from the deserts of Mongolia. So you may not need lots of water to drink, but you still need *some*."

"Mongolia?" said Jake as he squeezed out of the wall. "Is that *up*town or *down*town?"

"And you need to know *how* to drink too," said Molly.

"Gosh, I already know how to drink," said Dexter. "You don't have to teach me that!"

"What you know is how to drink from a bottle hanging upside down in a cage. It's a little different out here," instructed Molly. "Listen. Hear that drip, drip sound?"

Dexter cocked his ears and replied, "Yeah, what is it?"

"A leaky pipe high up on the ceiling. It drips down onto the floor behind a big oil tank where the janitor can't reach to fix it."

Jake wasn't all that interested in being Dexter's teacher. But he was very thirsty.

"Come on," he said, and led the way behind the tank to a circle of wet cement beneath the leaky pipe.

"Wow!" said Dexter as a falling drop of water sent a spritz of spray onto his face. "It's like having your own private waterfall!"

"That's why you have to be careful when you take a drink, or you could end up taking a shower, too," said Molly.

"Here, I'll show you how it's done," said Jake, and he stepped forward, looked up and opened his mouth. Out of the corner of his eye he could see a drip clinging to the pipe. For a moment it trembled, as if it were afraid to fall. Then it let go, gathering speed on its downward plunge.

Finally, *splash!* It collided with Jake's tongue.

Jake's face got a little wet, but most of the drop gushed down his throat into his belly.

"Now you try," said Molly.

As Jake stepped back Dexter stepped forward, looked up, and waited while another drop formed on the pipe.

"This takes a lot of patience, doesn't it?" he said, turning to Jake.

"Better pay attention!" said Molly.

Just then a big drop landed right on Dexter's nose. *Splat!*

Dexter just laughed, but all that got him was another drop between the ears. Then three more drops caught him on the neck and back. By the time Dexter had tasted even half a drop of water, he was sopping wet.

"Oh, well, I guess I needed a bath." Dexter grinned as he turned to lick his belly.

Molly shook her head disapprovingly.

"This is *not* a funny matter. If you want to live free like us, you've got to learn the proper way of getting a drink *without* getting wet."

"Oh, come on! You're taking all the fun out of this," said Dexter, and he sent a grin in Jake's direction as if to say, *Aren't girls silly?*

"You don't understand," insisted Molly. "It's October now and getting colder every day. Soon it will be winter. And you don't want to get wet in the wintertime."

"I don't?" said Dexter.

"No, you don't," said Molly. "Just think what could happen if you caught a chill and it turned into pneumonia? If you were a class pet, Miss Clark might take you to a vet. But out here, on your own, you could be dead in a day or two."

Finally Dexter stopped grinning.

"Let me show you where to dry off quick, in case you ever have to," said Molly.

The place to dry off was in front of the school furnace, which was located in the janitor's workshop.

On the way there Molly took Jake aside.

"I'm worried about Dexter," she said. "I'm afraid he doesn't have the right attitude to make it on his own."

"Then why bother to teach him anything?" said Jake. "Chances are he won't last a week."

"But you saw how he ran from those kids," said Molly. "He's quick and smart. If only you'd help me. Maybe we could—"

"Hey, what's that delicious smell?" called Dexter as he turned the corner.

Jake looked at Dexter as if he had just pulled out his tail and reattached it to the middle of his forehead. Then he remembered that Dexter had never eaten cheese.

"That *smell* is cheese," he announced, and sniffed. "Slightly aged Swiss cheese to be exact."

Dexter inhaled deeply and savored the aroma until his mouth began to water. "Wow! That's really something! I could just sit here and smell it all night long."

"If you think it smells good, wait till you taste it," said Molly, and she led Dexter down the hall and around the corner to a thick wooden door.

"This is the door to Mr. Hobbs's workshop," said Molly as she pressed her belly to the floor and prepared to slip under the door. "He's the janitor."

"Janitor?"

"That's the guy who does all the odd jobs around school like changing lightbulbs, cleaning windows, sweeping floors and—"

"Killing mice," added Jake as he followed Molly under the door. "Don't forget that one."

Mr. Hobbs's workshop was a narrow room with no windows. Its floor was covered with sawdust and scraps of wood, and its walls and shelves were cluttered with brooms and buckets and mops.

In the center of the room was a tall workbench. Beneath the workbench on the floor was a large wooden mousetrap. The spring was set. The trigger was ready. And the bait was a large cube of slightly aged Swiss cheese.

Molly and Jake, having grown up in a deli, were

fine judges of cheese. "Not the really expensive kind," assessed Jake with a single sniff.

"But not your cheap grocery-store variety either," said Molly.

"Cheap or expensive, it sure smells great to me," said Dexter as he walked up to the trap. "But what a strange dish it's on."

Strange dish? All of a sudden Molly realized Dexter didn't know what a mousetrap was.

"Stop!" she cried.

"Don't worry, I won't take more than my share," said Dexter, and he leaned forward and opened his mouth. "Just a nibble."

Molly nearly fainted with shock but Jake sprang into action. With the speed of a lizard's tongue, he scooped up the nearest object at hand—half a walnut shell—and leaped toward the trap. His idea was to place the shell on the trap between Dexter and the lethal execution bar, which was already arcing toward Dexter's neck.

Snap!

The trap resounded with an ear-splitting crack.

Chapter 4

Jake's quick reflexes saved Dexter's life. The bar came down on the walnut shell, not Dexter's neck. But the shell itself was not strong enough to absorb the full impact of the blow. When it cracked and gave way, both Dexter and Jake were pinned beneath the bar of the trap.

For a split second Dexter imagined that something like a firecracker or gun had gone off. *Is someone shooting at us?* he wondered. Then he felt a sharp horrible pain flash across his back.

"What happened!!!?" Dexter tried to say more, but the air was temporarily knocked out of his lungs.

"Yumping Yarlsburg!" gasped Jake. "I can't *believe* what you just did!"

"How was I supposed to know the dish was booby-trapped?" whined Dexter.

"You're the booby!" cried Jake as he winced with pain. "And this is no dish. It's a mousetrap! Haven't you ever heard of a mousetrap before? I mean, where have you been all your life?"

"You know where he's been!" said Molly as she quickly regained her composure, jumped onto the trap, and grabbed hold of the metal bar with both paws. "Don't move!"

" I *can't* move!" cried Dexter. "I'm stuck!"

"Don't even *try* to move," said Molly. "If the shell

gives way any more, the bar will crush you both!"

"Molly, what are you trying to do?" gasped Jake.

"I'm not sure," replied Molly. "But I thought maybe if all three of us lift together . . ."

"Good idea, sis," said Jake. "Okay, on the count of three we lift. One, two . . ."

Dexter and Jake strained to push up against the bar and Molly put all her muscle into lifting. But the bar wouldn't budge until Molly put her shoulder *under* it. Only then did it begin to rise.

"It's working!" cried Jake.

"Just a little more!" squeaked Molly.

But Dexter panicked. Instead of lifting with Molly and Jake until the bar was all the way up, he tried to scoot free too soon. In his haste he bumped the walnut shell aside and the bar slammed down.

"Ooof!" cried Molly as her paws flew out from beneath her.

Now Jake, Dexter, *and* Molly were pinned to the trap like three butterflies pinned to a corkboard.

"Thanks a lot, Dexter!" cried Jake as he strained under the renewed pressure of the metal bar.

"Sorry," whined Dexter. "I was only trying . . ."

"Never mind," said Molly. "I'm the teacher here. I should have warned you about mousetraps."

Jake made a disgusted face, looked away, and said nothing.

"So now what do we do?" cried Dexter.

"The only thing we can do," said Molly. "Wait."

"Wait for what?"

"Wait for morning when Mr. Hobbs comes to check his trap," answered Molly.

"Then what?"

"Then we either escape or die," said Jake.

A sliver of cheese was still in Dexter's mouth. Without thinking he chewed and swallowed it.

"So, how do you like *cheese*?" asked Molly.

"Pretty good," replied Dexter glumly.

"Good enough to die for?" asked Jake.

"No, not that good," said Dexter. "But almost," and he took another bite. "Want some?"

Chapter 5

Wake up!" cried Molly. "He's here!"
"Oh, my aching bones!" groaned Jake. "I dreamed I climbed a mountain with a rock as big as a watermelon tied to my back."

As soon as Dexter's eyes opened he winced with pain.

"I wish you hadn't woken me up," he moaned. "It was better when I was asleep."

"You can't sleep now," said Molly. "Mr. Hobbs is coming."

Jake's large leafy ears pricked up.

"Are you sure it's him?"

"Of course I'm sure!" said Molly. "I heard his key turn in the front door."

Mr. Hobbs was always the first to arrive every morning at P.S. 42, and the clunking sound of his heavy work boots was unmistakable.

"That's him all right," said Jake.

"What's he doing?" asked Dexter.

"What he does every morning," answered Jake. "First he'll check the thermostats and turn on the hall lights. Then he'll come down here."

"Then what?"

"Then hopefully he'll think we're all dead and throw us in the trash," said Molly.

"That's the good news?" gasped Dexter.

"You bet it is," said Molly. "I thought this all out while you two were snoozing. What we have to do is play dead. Once we're in the trash we can just chew our way out and escape back into the wall."

"So far so good, Sis," said Jake. "But what if Mr. Hobbs doesn't throw us in the trash? What if he tosses us in the furnace instead?"

"Then we switch to Plan B and make a run for it."

"Wait a minute," said Dexter. "Mr. Hobbs is trying to kill *you* guys. Not me. Once he sees I'm a gerbil, not a mouse, won't he want to return me to Miss Clark's class?"

"There's just one little problem with that." Molly scrunched up her face in an expression of pained regret. "Mr. Hobbs has *very* bad eyesight. He's lucky if he can tell the difference between a turtle and a tarantula, let alone a gerbil and a mouse."

"But won't he be on the lookout for an escaped class pet?" said Dexter desperately.

"Impossible," said Jake. "Yesterday was Tuesday. That's the day Mr. Hobbs always leaves early. So there's no way he could know about you and your escape."

"When you ran away you gave up all the rights and privileges of a class pet. Now, for better or worse, you're one of us," said Molly sternly. "So you better do exactly what we tell you to do. One slip up and you kill us all!"

"Do you understand what Molly just said?" asked Jake through a clenched jaw. "It's *very* important!"

"Yeah, I got it!" said Dexter, and he muttered

under his breath. "My first day of freedom and already I'm doomed."

"Now listen up!" said Molly. "We don't have a lot of time. As soon as Mr. Hobbs comes in we freeze. Don't move a whisker. Don't even breathe unless you absolutely have to."

"What about the tongue trick?" asked Jake.

"Good idea," said Molly.

"Tongue trick?" asked Dexter. "What's that?"

"It's something our poppa taught us," said Molly. "All you have to do is stick out your tongue." Molly stuck out her tongue and let it go limp out of the side of her mouth. "It will make you look more dead."

"Like this?" Dexter stuck out his tongue as if he were making a face at Molly.

"No, no, not that way." Molly ignored Dexter's childish insult. "Like this!"

It took Dexter a couple of tries, but he finally mastered the tongue trick.

"Excellent!" said Jake. "If I didn't know better I'd guess you've been dead for hours!"

"Which is exactly how I feel," moaned Dexter.

Mr. Hobbs's footsteps got louder as he descended the basement stairs.

"Remember," said Molly. *"Don't move! Don't breathe! Play dead!"*

The footsteps stopped. Then they heard the jingle of keys and the squeak of door hinges.

"Here he comes. Tongues out!"

Dexter froze the instant Mr. Hobbs came in the door. But he couldn't help sneaking a peek. Except for his boots, which were brown, Mr. Hobbs wore green pants, a green shirt, a green cap, and very large eye-glasses. In short, he looked like someone trying to impersonate a large nearsighted shrub.

"What's this?" Mr. Hobbs squinted and bent forward. "Three mice in one trap! This must be my lucky day!" Mr. Hobbs set down his lunch box and nudged Jake's body with the steel-reinforced toe of his boot. "I'd say you've eaten your last piece of *my* cheese, fellah!"

Mr. Hobbs bent down, picked up the trap, and started walking toward the furnace.

Dangling in midair, half on and half off the trap, neither Jake nor Molly nor Dexter made the slightest move to betray the fact that they were still alive. But they all stole quick glances to see where they were going.

"Looks like he's taking us to the furnace!" said Jake.

"Get ready to switch to Plan B," whispered Molly. "As soon as he lifts the bar we scram!"

"I'm not ready to die!" cried Dexter.

"Stop whining!" snapped Jake. "We're not dead yet."

"That's right," said Molly. "This could turn out to be *our* lucky day."

Mr. Hobbs stopped at the furnace, shook his head, and turned toward the trash barrel.

"See, what did I tell you?" said Molly. "He's going to throw us in the trash after all."

But Mr. Hobbs only stopped long enough to pull a small rag from the trash barrel. Then he proceeded past his jigsaw and paint table toward the bathroom.

"What's he doing now?" asked Dexter. Dexter's heart was beating so fast and loud, he was afraid Mr. Hobbs would hear it.

Holding the trap in his left hand, Mr. Hobbs lifted the toilet bowl seat with his right.

"I think he's going to flush us down the toilet!" cried Molly. "Get ready to make a run for it."

"Oh, mouse! I think you're right," exclaimed Jake.

Using the rag he'd taken from the trash, Mr. Hobbs slowly lifted the bar of the trap.

How insulting! thought Molly. *He doesn't even want to* touch *us.*

As soon as the bar was lifted from her shoulders Molly took in a deep breath and squeaked, *"Now!"* And they all pushed off from the trap.

Mr. Hobbs's eyebrows arched into a forehead wrinkled with outrage and surprise.

"Why you little fakers!" he cried.

Dexter slipped and went more or less straight down into the bowl. Jake managed to clear the rim of the toilet seat, but bounced off the lid. A moment after Dexter landed in the water, Jake splashed down beside him.

Only Molly managed to clear the rim of the toilet and fall to the floor.

"You won't get far!" cried Mr. Hobbs, and he quickly flushed the toilet, grabbed a toilet plunger, and went after Molly.

Chapter 6

Jake and Dexter spun around and around, as if riding on a merry-go-round made of water.

"I can't swim! I can't swim!" he sputtered.

Jake couldn't swim much either and was taking in huge mouthfuls of water. But he called out to Dexter, "Hold on to my tail!"

Already a vertical funnel had formed and was beginning to suck them down.

"These survival lessons have been great!" Dexter shouted above the gurgling gush of water. "But I don't think I'll be able to make the next class."

"Don't give up," said Jake. "My uncle Ralph was flushed down the toilet fourteen times. The owner of the house where he lived thought he had a mouse infestation. But it was just Uncle Ralph getting caught again and again. If Uncle Ralph, who was fat and old, could survive fourteen flushings, then we can make it just this once!"

"How did he survive?" Dexter wanted to know. "Did he have some kind of secret?"

"You bet he did," cried Jake.

"Well? What was it?" Dexter took in a big mouthful of water and spat it out.

"At the very last moment before he went down" — Jake sputtered as a wave of water slapped him in the face— "he took in a big gulp of air and held his breath!"

"That's it? That's Uncle Ralph's secret?"

"That's it!" cried Jake. "It's not fancy, but it works. So just stay calm and I'll tell you when to take in that big gulp of air."

The current was getting stronger now. It opened up from beneath and engulfed them in a dizzy blur. Round and round they spun like two whirling dervishes.

"Now?" called Dexter.

"Almost," cried Jake. "On the count of three. Ready, one, two, three!"

Suddenly there was a loud, hollow, gushing sound.

The water spun them so fast, like a high-speed drill.

More than anything Dexter wanted to scream, but instead he pumped his lungs with air and tightened his grip on Jake's tail.

Then all of a sudden he felt himself spiraling into a bottomless dive!

Sucked down, and then up and around a tight bend in the plumbing, Jake and Dexter sloshed out of P.S. 42 and into the sewer lines beneath the streets. Small pipes led to larger ones and those pipes dumped them into still larger ones. Twists and bends and countless right-angled turns were accomplished in one long, wet, dark, swoosh!

Finally the two waterlogged rodents were dumped into a very large cement pipe only half-filled with water. Here the current slowed and they were able to rise to the surface.

Flinging back their heads, they gorged themselves on air, sucking it down their throats in big gulps.

Staying afloat was not easy with Dexter clinging to him, but Jake managed to swim to the edge of the

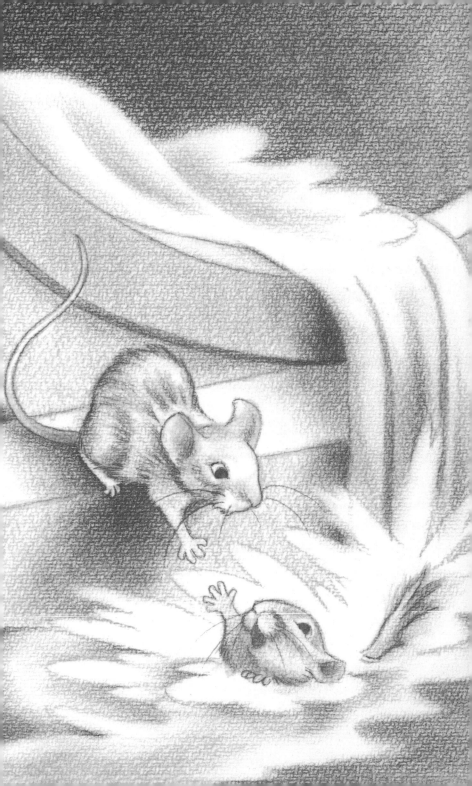

pipe and found a ledge that ran just above the water line.

Grabbing hold of the rough cement with his paws, Jake pulled himself up out of the current and onto the ledge. Then he reached down and gave Dexter a paw up.

For a long while the soggy survivors lay on their bellies panting, while an endless stream of foul-smelling sewage flowed past.

"What a stink!" groaned Dexter.

"Worse than cafeteria puke!" replied Jake with a grin, "but I'm sure glad we're alive to smell it!"

"And I'm glad your uncle Ralph told you his secret!"

"Uncle Ralph?" Jake looked confused. "Oh yeah! My uncle Ralph." He chuckled. "Actually, I don't have an Uncle Ralph. I just made him up."

Dexter was stunned.

"His secret, too? You made that up?"

"That's right," said Jake. "I was afraid you'd panic and drown us both, so I gave you something to hold on to besides me."

"So survival school is still in session?" said Dexter with a weary smile.

Jake had not wanted to get involved in Molly's survival school. But there was no avoiding it now.

"You bet it is," he replied. "And from the looks of this place, I'd say we've *both* got a lot to learn."

Chapter 7

Whack! Whack! Whack! The plunger struck so close and hard, Molly could feel the concrete floor vibrate beneath her paws. More than once its hard rubber cup almost crushed her, but somehow she managed to zigzag and dodge her way out of the bathroom.

"Rotten rodents!" cursed Mr. Hobbs, and he threw the plunger down and picked up a hockey stick. One of P.S. 42's older students had asked him to fix it for him. But now Mr. Hobbs didn't care if he smashed it.

Bam! Bam! Bam! Again and again the hockey stick came down like a meat cleaver. But it only nicked the tip of Molly's tail.

Disappearing into the clutter wasn't difficult. But Mr. Hobbs, intent upon Molly's destruction, started moving objects aside one at a time.

If only I can get to the door! thought Molly.

As Mr. Hobbs's search-and-destroy mission got closer and closer, Molly moved from one hiding place to another. She ran from a floor buffer to a shovel, from the shovel to a can of wax and a bucket of bolts. Then she saw an old golf ball on the floor beside her and got an idea. When Mr. Hobbs lifted the bucket, instead of running, Molly gave the golf ball a hefty shove.

The ball rolled across the workshop floor, and Mr. Hobbs turned to chase it.

Hoping this was the break she needed, Molly bee-lined it to the door. But halfway there . . .

Thwack!

The hockey stick came down like a bolt of lightning.

Mr. Hobbs may be old and half blind, but he sure is quick, thought Molly.

In her panic Molly gave up on the door for the moment, and slipped between two metal filing cabinets.

Good! she thought, panting from the chase. *It's dark back here. Now if I can scoot along the wall, maybe I can make it to the door after all.*

But the backs of the cabinets were flush against the wall.

Oops! Dead end!

Molly spun around to retrace her steps. But it was too late. Mr. Hobbs had already closed off the entrance between the two cabinets with a block of wood.

The walls of the cabinet were too high to jump and too slick to climb.

"Trapped!" squeaked Molly.

Mr. Hobbs's pockmarked face loomed above her like some sinister moon in a horror movie. For a full minute he peered down at her, his huge eyes swimming back and forth behind their fishbowl lenses like two huge brown guppies. Then suddenly a toothy smile spread across Mr. Hobbs's face.

Uh-oh! thought Molly. *He's got an idea, and judging from that ugly grin, it's not a friendly one.*

Molly was right. Mr. Hobbs did have an idea. And it was anything but friendly.

Shoving aside a workbench, he put his shoulders to one of the cabinets and began to push. The cabinet held heavy metal tools, pipes, and boxes of nails. So it moved slowly, inch by inch, screeching as it scraped against the cement floor.

Mr. Hobbs was only strong enough to move one end of the cabinet at a time. Every time the cabinet budged a little, he grunted. *Screech!* Grunt! *Screech!* Grunt! With each screech and grunt the valley between the two cabinets became narrower and narrower.

"He's going to squish me!" squeaked Molly. "He's going to squish me like a bug!"

Chapter 8

"Well, Teach," said Dexter. "Now that I passed the toilet flush test, what's next?"

"What's next is getting out of this sewer." Jake stood up and sniffed in several directions. "It's not as strong as some of the other smells down here, but the scent of rat is everywhere."

Dexter stood up on his hind legs and sniffed also.

"It doesn't smell like the rats I remember from Pretty Pets."

"And they don't act like them either," said Jake. "Sewer rats are bad news. Almost as bad as cats."

Jake stared downstream and squinted. "See that light ahead of us? I think that's our way out."

The light was very faint, but brightened as they walked toward it. After a while the pipe they were in joined with another, larger pipe. This pipe had no water in it, just rocks and twigs and other odd pieces of debris.

Since Jake mentioned sewer rats, Dexter could think of nothing else. All he wanted to do was get out of the sewer and feel some real sunlight on his fur. As he walked beside Jake he remembered the day the owner of Pretty Pets had put the gerbil tank in the front window, and how great it had felt to stretch out and bask in the sun. It was a soothing memory, but it didn't help much to ease the pain in his back or the chill of his wet fur. And it didn't help him shake the creepy feeling that sewer rats could be lurking around the next bend.

Suddenly Jake stopped and sniffed. Up ahead was a sharp turn in the pipe, and beyond that the light seemed brighter.

"What are we stopping for?"

"Shhhhh!" Jake crept slowly toward the turn in the pipe.

Dexter followed silently until Jake stopped again.

"Just as I thought," whispered Jake. "Sewer rats! A whole pack of them. We probably should turn around. But they're standing right next to the exit. Take a look."

Jake pulled back so Dexter could edge forward and see around the bend.

The exit was there, all right. Bright slashes of sunlight fell from a street grate above. It would be so easy to crawl up the concrete pipe and through the metal grate. Dexter yearned to be free of this dark, smelly place. But the rats were gathered almost directly below the grate. And they were ghastly!

Seven or eight hulking rat monsters were crowded around a severed fish head. Only one rat, twice as large as any of the others, was eating it. This rat had long brownish teeth, a gnarled face with mean, narrow eyes, and scars all up and down his back.

"Come on, Bruce," said one of the smaller rats. "Give us a taste, why don't you?"

"I'll give you a taste you won't forget!" snarled the huge rat called Bruce, and he whipped around and lashed out at his challenger.

It happened so fast, all Dexter saw was a blur. Then Bruce was back chewing on his fish head, and the smaller rat was bleeding just below his shoulder.

"I've seen enough," said Dexter. "I say we go back and find some other way out."

"Too late for that," said Jake.

Behind him Dexter heard the sound of paws on concrete. Then several rat-shaped shadows appeared on the walls of the pipe. Another pack of rats was approaching. It was impossible to count their numbers, but this pack looked even larger than the one under the grate.

"Now what?" said Dexter. "Are these rats going to want to beat us up?"

"Beat us up, nothing!" snapped Jake. "They're going to want to *eat* us, bones and all!"

"Eat us?" Dexter trembled. "What are we going to do?"

At this point Jake had only a vague plan. But that didn't stop him from taking charge.

"Just follow me," he said. "Do what I do. But don't say a word. I'll do all the talking."

"Okay," said Dexter, and he pulled himself together as best he could.

Jake waited until the other rat pack got a little closer. Then he jumped out from behind the bend and ran toward Bruce and his pack, shouting, "Poppa! Poppa! Save us!"

Bruce could see at a glance that Jake was *not* his son. Or even a rat for that matter. But Jake's outrageous lie distracted him enough to sidetrack his instinct to kill now and ask questions later.

Taking advantage of Bruce's confusion, Jake cried out. "Big rats! Almost bigger than you, Poppa! And they're coming to kill us!"

Jake had guessed correctly that Bruce's size was a point of pride for him.

"What? Bigger than me? There's no rat bigger than me!"

By now Bruce and his pack were galvanized for a major rat war. As they moved forward toward the approaching rat pack, Jake and Dexter slipped past them toward the grate.

Chapter 9

creech! Grunt! *Screech!* Grunt! The space between the cabinets shrunk to just two inches, then just one.

One more shove and Molly would be squished as flat as a pancake. Not roadkill, but cabinetkill.

Then the wooden board blocking her exit fell to the floor.

This is it! My last chance!

Molly made a desperate dash for the opening.

But that was exactly what Mr. Hobbs expected her to do. As she shot out from between the two cabinets a bucket came down over her head with a resounding clank.

"Gotcha!" cried Mr. Hobbs.

Molly banged her head on the bucket and fell down. For a moment everything went dim. Then she sat up and realized she had been tricked.

That piece of wood didn't fall over! Mr. Hobbs pushed it over, and I ran right into his trap!

In the darkness under the bucket Molly could hear the toilet refilling with water. *I guess it doesn't matter what happens to me now,* she thought. *Jake is already gone! And that poor, poor Dexter . . .*

After searching around his workshop for a minute or so, Mr. Hobbs lifted the bucket just enough to slide a piece of cardboard under its rim. As it came toward

her Molly had no choice but to hop on top of it.

If ever there were a hopeless situation, this is it, thought Molly. *It's only a matter of time now, before Mr. Hobbs throws me away like an old peanut shell.*

But Molly was not a quitter. As Mr. Hobbs lifted the cardboard and bucket off the floor Molly knew she would fight to the end.

If I get the chance, I'll bite him! she thought. *I'll bite him hard!*

Suddenly Mr. Hobbs turned Molly's prison upside down, and she fell with a clunk to the bottom of the bucket. The cardboard floor she had been standing on was now her ceiling. Slowly it slid to one side, just far enough to allow a sliver of light into the bucket. As Molly peered upward through the light she saw Mr. Hobbs's right eyeball staring down at her.

"Two down, one to go," said Mr. Hobbs.

Then the crack closed and Molly felt the bucket lift into the air.

He must be taking me to the toilet, she thought. *Watery death, here I come.*

Molly heard the screech of metal hinges. *What's that? Certainly not the toilet.*

Again the cardboard slid back, this time not just a crack, but all the way.

Molly's instinct was to jump. Then she felt a wave of heat and the glare of hot yellow flames.

Molly was nowhere near the toilet. Mr. Hobbs had taken her to the furnace and was about to throw her in.

"Time to go," he said, and slowly tilted the bucket toward the furnace door.

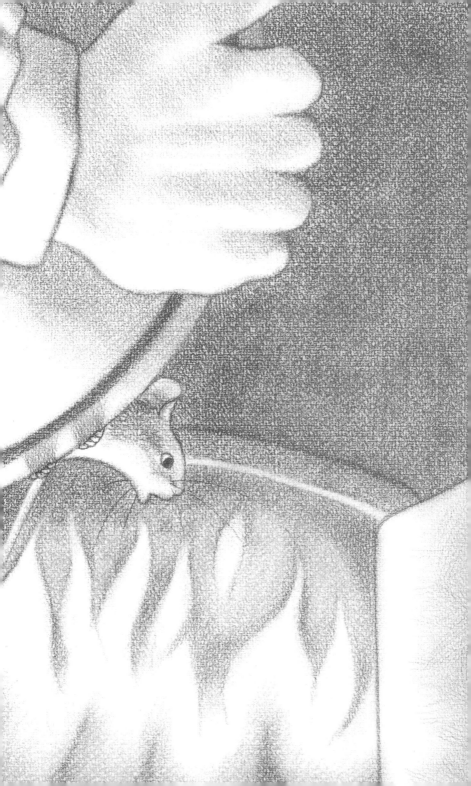

Chapter 10

Breathless from the mad dash past the rat pack, Dexter clung to the grate beside Jake.

"What . . ." It took him a while to get the words out. "Are . . . we . . . stopping for?"

"Take a look."

Dexter stuck his head up out of the grate and was confronted by an endless procession of cars and pedestrians—morning rush-hour traffic in full swing.

"We can't just dash out there," said Jake. "It would be suicide!"

Dexter looked down and saw the two packs of rats gathering beneath them.

"But the rats . . . they're not fighting each other," he said breathlessly. "They're coming after us!"

"Clever mice!" snarled Bruce from below. "Thought you could trick us, eh?"

"Come on, boys! Let's get 'em!" said the leader of the other pack.

Just then Jake saw an old man pushing a hot dog cart turn the corner and head for the grate.

"We'll wait till that cart rolls over us," said Jake. "Then we'll jump out and run beneath it. As long as we stay under the cart we'll be safe."

"Wait? Are you crazy?" cried Dexter. "Bruce and his pals are coming to get us!"

"Go ahead. Run if you want to," said Jake. "I'm waiting."

Dexter looked down and saw a swarm of hungry rat eyes getting closer and closer. Snarling and hissing and lusting after mouse meat, in a matter of seconds the rats would be upon them.

But Jake held fast. And Dexter stood by his side until the hot dog cart rattled over the grate.

"Now!" cried Jake.

Just then Bruce, leading the attack, took a swipe at Dexter.

But Dexter dodged his blow and leaped out of the grate onto the street just behind Jake.

"Watch out for those wheels!" cried Jake as the two rodents ran side by side under the shadow of the cart.

Behind them Bruce stuck his head out of the grate.

"You'd better run, you lousy runts!" he shouted after them.

Jake wished he could think of some clever retort, but the only word that came to him as he turned and called out over his shoulder was, "Loser!"

"And just for your information, I'm not a mouse," added Dexter gleefully. "I'm a gerbil!"

"I don't care what you are," spat Bruce. "Come back to my sewer again and I'll swallow you both in one gulp!" Then the angry rat ducked down to avoid the tires of a passing taxi.

After the dank, smelly confines of the sewer, the sunshine and fresh air made Jake and Dexter feel giddy.

"I never liked running in exercise wheels," declared Dexter happily. "But this feels great!"

"Just stick with me, pal, and you'll never have to run in an exercise wheel again!" boasted Jake.

After a full block of running, both Dexter and Jake began to tire. The hot dog cart had provided an excellent means of escape from the sewer, but now they were stuck under the cart. They couldn't just stop because the hot dog vendor might step on them. And the wheels of the cart might run them over if they tried to scoot out ahead or to either side.

Dexter was the first to run out of steam. "What now?" he panted.

"Just keep running, I guess," said Jake.

"I'm sure glad he's an old guy," said Dexter. "If he went any faster I couldn't keep up."

"He must be going *somewhere*," huffed Jake. "He'll have to stop soon."

The vendor crossed a wide avenue and turned down a narrow street that suddenly looked and smelled very familiar to Jake.

"Oh, Mighty Mouse!" he cried. "This is the street I grew up on. And look over there! That's Deli Dan's!"

The hot dog vendor not only walked by Deli Dan's, he stopped in front of it and parked his cart. Then he went inside to buy a few extra cartons of hot dog rolls.

"I couldn't run a single step more!" Dexter collapsed onto the pavement and rolled over on his back to inspect his paws. "Look at these! Do they look red to you?"

Jake was too excited to rest.

"Come on." He scooted around the wheels of the cart and dashed across the sidewalk into the alley beside Deli Dan's.

"Hey, wait for me." Dexter picked himself up and followed behind, panting.

Once in the relative safety of the alley, Jake waded into a puddle and began to wash himself off. "I just can't believe that hot dog vendor led us back to Deli Dan's," said Jake as he scrubbed behind his ears. "This *is* my lucky day!"

"I'm sorry, but getting flushed down the toilet and chased by rats all before breakfast is not my idea of a *lucky* day," said Dexter.

"You don't understand," said Jake. "This is where I grew up. This is my *home!*"

"I guess I don't," sighed Dexter. "I grew up at Pretty Pets and that's the last place I'd *ever* want to visit."

"Come on. Wash off. I don't want us smelling like poop when we meet my folks."

"No problem," said Dexter, and he also waded into the puddle and began to wash.

Soon mouse and gerbil were dunking and shaking like two sparrows.

"Smell me," said Jake when he emerged from the puddle.

"Better," said Dexter with a quick sniff. Then he made a face. "But not much."

"I guess that can't be helped. It will probably take days for this stench to really wear off. This way," said Jake, and he led Dexter through a broken basement window into Deli Dan's.

Chapter 11

Hot flames licked Molly's fur as she clung to the rim of the bucket. In another moment she would have to let go and fall to a fiery death. But just then the school intercom clicked on.

"Oh, Mr. Hobbs!" The fluty, musical voice of Mrs. Wiser, the school principal, pierced the air like an irritating door buzzer. "Are you *there*, Mr. Hobbs?"

Mr. Hobbs looked up at the speaker mounted above the doorway of his workshop.

"If this is about the light in the front hall, I located the right bulb and—"

"No, no," said Mrs. Wiser. "This is about something Miss Clark wanted you to know. She stopped by my office after school yesterday and told me to tell you first thing in the morning that her new class pet has escaped. She wants you to be on the lookout for it and take in any mousetraps you may have set out."

"Sure thing, Mrs. Wiser. What kind of pet is it?"

"It's a gerbil," said Mrs. Wiser.

"Gerbil, you say?" Mr. Hobbs squinted down at Molly and tilted the bucket away from the furnace.

"That's right," said Mrs. Wiser. "And Mr. Hobbs . . ."

"Yes, Mrs. Wiser."

"The front hall *is* very dark without a light. It would be wonderful if the bulb could be replaced sometime soon . . . Like today, perhaps? One of the parents complained about it last night."

The PA system clicked off and Mr. Hobbs's workshop suddenly seemed very quiet.

"Well, well, well!" Mr. Hobbs looked down at Molly and smiled. "Gerbil, eh? I guess I better have a closer look at you."

"Better look fast!" cried Molly. "I'm out of here!"

Just as Molly sprang to leap out of the bucket, Mr. Hobbs replaced the cardboard.

Thud!

Molly smashed her head and fell to the bottom of the bucket.

On a tall wooden shelf at the back of his workshop sat an old aquarium Mr. Hobbs had rescued from the trash many years ago.

"I knew this would come in handy someday," he mumbled to himself as he took the aquarium down and set it on his workbench. The tank was encrusted with dirt and grime. But with a few squirts of window cleaner and some quick work with paper towels, Mr. Hobbs soon had it looking like new.

Then the hard-working janitor lifted Molly's bucket, dumped her in the aquarium, and slapped a small window screen on top.

"Now we'll take a good look at you." Mr. Hobbs sat down on a tall stool and, placing his elbows on his workbench, leaned forward.

As Molly looked up at Mr. Hobbs she saw a strange transformation take place. The hard look in his eyes disappeared and was replaced with a softer, almost childlike gleam.

"I had a pet when I was a kid," he said to Molly. "Not like you at all. He was a dog, a big dog, named Captain . . . a mutt really."

Mr. Hobbs's eyes seemed to cloud over as he drifted inward and back in time.

"I found Captain on the street and gave him a home for a long time," Mr. Hobbs paused and wiped his hands across his face. "When we moved I couldn't keep him anymore. I had to give him to a friend. Captain was a *great* watchdog. Never bit nobody, but he sure barked a lot."

Mr. Hobbs reached over, pulled his lunch pail toward him, lifted the latch, and opened it.

"Let's see. What do we have here?" he said, folding back a plastic bag.

Molly heard crinkle sounds and smelled cheese.

She thought Mr. Hobbs was going to have a snack for himself. She never dreamed he would offer *her* any.

"You've had a rough night, haven't you?"

Mr. Hobbs opened one of his sandwiches and broke off a piece of cheese. Then he lifted the screen and dropped the cheese into the aquarium.

Molly was hungry and the cheese smelled good. She went over to it and took a nibble.

"Good, eh?" Mr. Hobbs smiled at her.

Molly wanted to feel good toward Mr. Hobbs. It was plain to see he wasn't really such a bad guy after all. Then she realized the cheese she was eating was slightly aged Swiss, the same kind of cheese Mr. Hobbs had used to murder her brother!

Chapter 12

Deli Dan's was just as Jake remembered it. All the old familiar smells were there. The aromas of sauerkraut, corned beef and cabbage, cheeses of all kinds, sausage, salami, and pickle brine—all mixed together—made Jake feel at home.

"Is that you, Jake?" Uncle Louie, the rat, called out from behind a broken box of oyster crackers. "Well, cross the equator in a teacup!" The old fellow stood up on his hind legs and sniffed. "You smell like you' been sailing in the sewers!"

Uncle Louie was the only rat that lived at Deli Dan's. He never bothered the mice that lived upstairs and they never minded him in the least. In fact, all the young mice adored him because Uncle Louie once lived on a ship and had all kinds of daring sea-faring yarns to share.

"Hi, Uncle Louie!" Jake jumped from the window ledge straight down to the floor. Dexter followed, but he jumped from the window ledge, to a box of sardines *and then* to the floor.

"Who's your friend?" asked Uncle Louie.

"This is Dexter," said Jake as he greeted Uncle Louie with a nose touch. "He's a gerbil."

"Pleased to make your acquaintance, mate," said the scruffy brown rat with black markings on his back and forehead. "Any friend of Jake's is a friend of mine. Here, have a cracker." Uncle Louie thrust an oyster cracker into Dexter's paws.

"Gee, thanks," said Dexter. "I never had one of these."

"Take as many as you like!" said Uncle Louie, and he pushed some crackers in Jake's direction.

"Wow! These are good! These are *really* good!" Dexter quickly polished off one cracker and reached for another.

"Sure is good to see you, Uncle Louie," said Jake.

"Been a while since you shipped out," replied Uncle Louie. "What brings you back to this port?"

"Just visiting."

Jake gave the shortest of answers because more than anything he wanted to go upstairs and see his momma and poppa.

"Well, how's it been going? Smooth sailing?" asked Uncle Louie. "You and your sister all ship-shape?"

"Yep," said Jake. "We moved into a school."

"Your momma will be glad to hear that," said Uncle Louie. "She always wanted her children to get an education."

"Where are Momma and Poppa?" asked Jake, and for the first time noticed that something smelled different about the place. "They're okay, aren't they?"

"As fit as catnip!" said Uncle Louie. "I imagine they're still asleep in their kettle. We all had a meeting late last night. There's been some changes here at the deli since you left. In fact, I'd say you came at the *last possible moment*."

That sounded ominous to Jake.

"I'd like to hear more later, but right now I want to see Momma and Poppa." Jake asked Uncle Louie to look after Dexter for a while. "Up until now Dexter's never eaten anything but gerbil food."

"Run along, mate," said Uncle Louie. "I'll take your friend on a cook's tour."

Jake's parents slept in the back room of the deli in an old teakettle that lay on its side between a broken meat slicer and an empty pickle barrel.

Fond memories and warm feelings flooded Jake as he approached the tarnished vessel and tapped his paws on its spout.

"Momma, Poppa!" he called out, and there was a stirring inside.

"What is it?" came Poppa's familiar voice, and Jake's heart started thumping.

"It's me, Jake."

"Jake!" cried Momma, and almost immediately her head popped out of the spout.

Momma's eyes sparkled with love as she squeezed her plump body onto the floor. Then she rushed over to Jake. Instead of giving him the usual greeting among mice, a nose touch, she reached out and pulled him into a tight embrace. Jake's back was sore from having spent all night in the mousetrap. But he didn't mind his mother's squeeze in the least.

"My child! My baby! My pup!" Momma cried and shed huge tears, which fell and ran down Jake's back. Then she sniffed and pulled back. "Have you been living in the sewer?"

"No, Momma," said Jake. "But I used one to get here."

"Good," said Momma. "I won't have any of my kin living in the sewer. They're not safe. Never have been and never will be."

By then Jake's Poppa was out of the kettle as well.

"Let me have a look at you," said Poppa, and he, too, gave Jake a hug.

Nothing escaped Poppa's scrutiny. "You look like you had a rough night," he said. "From the smell of you I'd say you not only spent some time in the sewer recently, but you also had a close call with some sewer rats."

"That's right," said Jake, and he launched into a long story about everything that had happened to him and Molly since they left the deli.

"Molly is safe, isn't she?" asked Momma as soon as Jake mentioned her name. "Why didn't she come along?"

"I think she's safe," said Jake, and he recounted the events of the night before and explained how he hadn't intended to visit at all.

"That's just as well," said Poppa. "We mice had a meeting last night and decided by unanimous vote to leave the deli as soon as we find a place to resettle."

Jake never expected to hear such shocking news.

"Leave the deli? Why?"

Suddenly another mouse stuck its head out of the spout. It was Jake's youngest brother, Baby Ben.

"The monster!" cried Baby Ben. "That's why!"

"Hi, Benny!" said Jake as he helped his little brother out of the spout. "What monster are you talking about, something you saw in a dream?"

"He's no dream," said Baby Ben with a shiver. "He's a nightmare!"

"Baby Ben is right," said Poppa. "We are moving because of a monster, a monster cat that comes around every night. He sneaks in through the basement window and terrorizes everyone here. The only one not terrified of him is Uncle Louie."

"He's not like any ordinary cat on the prowl, looking for a meal or some mean amusement," said Momma. "He seems to have it in for us and won't rest until we're all destroyed. Already he's tangled with Uncle Howard and Cousin Rachel, and badly mauled Aunt Bernice."

Momma's words gave Jake a sinking feeling in the pit of his stomach.

"Is this cat big and gray, by any chance?" he asked.

"That's right," said Momma. "In fact, they call him—"

"No, don't tell me," said Jake. "They call him . . . Big Gray."

"You know him?" gasped Poppa.

"I'm afraid I do," confessed Jake. "The last time I had a run in with Big Gray, he swore to seek vengeance not only on me, but on my entire clan."

"So he hasn't chosen us at random," said Poppa. "I thought so!"

"What did you do to make him so angry?" asked Momma.

"I bit him," said Jake.

"You bit him!" squeaked Poppa. "Don't you know all cats *hate* that? It drives them absolutely insane for revenge. I'm sure as sugar I warned you about that!"

"You did," said Jake. "More than once. But it was either bite or die. So I bit."

"You did the right thing," said Momma, and she planted a consoling kiss on Jake's forehead.

"Thanks, Momma," said Jake with a heavy sigh. "But look at all the trouble I caused. If I had it to do over again, I might choose differently."

"There's no cheese in thinking like that," said Poppa. "The most important thing is to get out of here and get yourself back to that school as soon as possible. Big Gray sneaks into the deli at night, as soon as Deli Dan locks up. But some days he lurks about outside. When that cat smells your scent in this store, he's going to go after you no matter what."

"You're right," said Jake. "I should leave right away, but how can I go not knowing if you and Momma will be safe?"

"You could take us with you!" cried Baby Ben.

"Shush!" said Momma.

"Wait a minute," said Poppa. "That might not be a bad idea. Is this school of yours safe from cats?"

"Oh, yes," said Jake. "The janitor locks it up tight every night. That's probably why Big Gray has come after you. Because he can't get at *me* inside the school."

"And the food at the school?" asked Momma.

"Not as good as here," said Jake. "But we manage quite well."

Then Momma and Poppa looked at each other and, without saying a word, came to a decision.

"Then we'll go with you," said Poppa, and Momma nodded her assent.

"Oh, Mouse and double Mouse!" cried Jake. "That would be so great!"

"Maybe others would like to come too," suggested Momma.

Poppa thought for a moment. "After we've been to the school and seen what it's like we'll know better about that. Right now I think we should travel light. Just you, me, and Jake."

"What about me?" cried Baby Ben. "I can come too, can't I?"

"Of course you can!" said Momma. "We wouldn't leave you behind!" And she gave Baby Ben a warm hug.

Chapter 13

H i, Mr. Hobbs!" said a thin, high-pitched voice.
Mr. Hobbs turned and saw a small dark-haired
girl standing in his doorway. The girl wore blue jeans
and a white sweatshirt emblazoned with green and
purple teddy bears. In her hand she held a large pencil sharpener.

"Come on in," said Mr. Hobbs. "What can I do for
you?"

"My teacher, Mr. Blatterwort, told me to bring
this down to you," she said, holding out the pencil
sharpener. "He said you could fix it."

"I hope I can." Mr. Hobbs took the cover off the
sharpener and examined its workings with the small
magnifying glass he kept on a chain with his keys. All
the pencil sharpener seemed to need was a bit of
tightening. "Tell Mr. Blatterwort I'll drop it by after
lunch."

Mr. Hobbs turned away, expecting the girl to run
off. But she just stood there staring at Molly in the
aquarium.

"What's that?" she asked.

"Don't rightly know," said Mr. Hobbs. "Could be
a mouse or it could be Miss Clark's new class pet."

"It looks like a mouse to me," said the girl, step-
ping closer for a better look.

"That's what I thought," Mr. Hobbs said. "But I

seem to remember that gerbils look a lot like mice."

"I'll tell you if it's a gerbil or not," the girl said, and she stepped up onto the wooden toolbox beside Mr. Hobbs's workbench. "If it's a class pet it will be tame and easy to hold."

Before he could stop her, the girl shoved the screen aside and stuck her hand down in the aquarium.

"That's *not* a good idea!" protested Mr. Hobbs.

But the girl ignored him.

"Come on," she said to Molly softly. "I won't hurt you."

"Now, missy!" Mr. Hobbs raised his voice. "You really shouldn't do that!"

"Don't worry," the girl said. "I'm good with pets. We have a parakeet at home. His name is Safire. He bites everybody, even my dad. But he never even pecks at me."

Molly was still feeling sad about Jake. But she couldn't resist the chance to be picked up and held like a real class pet. Without a moment's hesitation she walked over to the little girl's hand and crawled into her soft sweaty palm. Then she brushed her face and whiskers against the little girl's thumb.

"I guess she must be a gerbil," said Mr. Hobbs. "I never saw a wild mouse act like that."

"I'd say so," the little girl said as she lifted Molly out of the aquarium and cuddled her in both hands next to her chest. "And she's sweet, too. Very sweet!"

What a feeling! thought Molly. *What a terrific feeling!* Molly closed her eyes and imagined herself floating in a pink cloud. The little girl's hands were

soft and warm and smelled so good. *Oh*, sighed Molly, *this is heaven!*

"Are you scared, little one?" asked the girl.

"Not now," squeaked Molly.

"Did you feed her, Mr. Hobbs?"

"Yes, I did," Mr. Hobbs replied. "Some cheese."

"Good," said the girl.

Molly popped her head up from between the little girl's fingers and looked up at Mr. Hobbs's face.

"Isn't she cute?"

"Very cute," replied Mr. Hobbs.

"She's more than cute," said the little girl as she stroked Molly's soft chestnut-colored fur. "She's adorable!"

"Yes," Molly said with a sigh as she basked in the warm glow of the little girl's love. "I'm *totally* adorable!"

"What's your name?" asked Mr. Hobbs.

"Ava," replied the little girl. "Ava Roberson-Rice."

"That's a nice name," said Mr. Hobbs.

"Here . . . you want to hold her?" Ava thrust Molly at Mr. Hobbs.

"That's okay," said Mr. Hobbs.

"Go ahead," said Ava. "She won't bite. She's sweet."

"I'm not afraid of her biting me," said Mr. Hobbs in a strong voice.

"Then go ahead," said Ava.

This time when Ava held Molly out to Mr. Hobbs, he opened his hands and cupped them around hers.

"That's it," said Ava. "That's the way to do it."

Molly preferred to stay with the little girl. But when Ava opened her hands and turned them upside down, she had no choice but to drop into Mr. Hobbs's hands.

Suddenly Mr. Hobbs's face lit up, and the little boy inside of him seemed to come alive.

"Her feet are cold and they tickle!" he said with a chuckle that was almost a giggle.

"You never held a gerbil before. Did you?" said Ava.

"I don't think so. No, never!" Mr. Hobbs replied.

"Well, there's always a first time, isn't there?" Ava said with a happy smile.

"Yep. There's always a first time," Mr. Hobbs said, and he reached over, broke off another piece of cheese from his sandwich, and fed Molly from his hand.

Chapter 14

Jake was terribly disappointed. He had hoped to visit at the deli for at least a day or two. Now there was hardly time to greet old friends and relatives before he had to leave.

Dexter was disappointed too. After the taste tour Uncle Louie gave him, he was ready to move into the deli for good.

"I don't understand!" he complained, almost begging. "Why can't I just stay here?"

"Because it's not safe," said Jake. "And let's face it. You're not ready to make it on your own. You *belong* in a cage."

Dexter heaved a heavy sigh and looked dejected. "I thought I was doing good."

"Have you forgotten about the mousetrap?" said Jake.

"Yeah, but now I know about mousetraps," argued Dexter. "That won't happen again ever!"

"Sure you do." Jake tried not to be harsh but he couldn't help himself. "And what about poison? If you want to live out here you've got to know which food is poison and which is not. Do you know *anything* about poison?"

"No," said Dexter with a sulk.

"And there's a lot more you don't know," said Jake. "The fact is you're a fatal accident waiting to happen, a danger to yourself and everyone you're around."

Jake hadn't intended to be mean, but his words cut deep.

"Look, it's not like you flunked out of survival school" —he tried to smooth things over— "in fact, lately you've gotten some pretty high grades. You just aren't ready to graduate yet, that's all."

"It's okay," Dexter said in a small hollow voice. "I understand." And he walked off to sit by himself in a corner and sulk.

"Do you know the way to the school from here?" Momma asked Jake.

"I think so," said Jake. "But last time Molly and I traveled there we traveled at night."

"Don't worry. I know every back alley route in town," said Poppa. "As long as Baby Ben doesn't slow us down we'll be just fine."

"What are you talking about?" protested Baby Ben. "I can run as fast as a cheater."

"You mean as fast as a cheetah," said Momma.

"Yeah, cheetah!"

"Sure you can," said Jake, and he gave Benny a brotherly cuff behind his ear.

After all the appropriate good-byes, hugs, kisses, and nose touches, Poppa said, "Now remember. If anything happens and we get split up, we'll meet at the edge of the park."

"Where's that?" said Baby Ben.

"Don't worry," said Momma. "Just stay close to me and you'll be fine."

Then Poppa led everyone out the basement window into the alley beside the store.

As soon as Jake stepped out into the alley he felt his whiskers tingle. *This alley would be a great place for an ambush,* he thought, and sniffed the morning air for any scent of danger. But the odor of spoiled produce, wilted lettuce, and empty tin cans that had once contained pork-and-beans blotted out any other smell that might have been there. *I'm just a little jumpy. That's all,* he thought.

Then Poppa stopped and sniffed too.

"Danger!" he cried. "Everyone, back to the deli!"

"Awww! Poppa! We just got going. Do we have to?" complained Baby Ben.

"Do as Poppa says!" Momma commanded, her voice full of concern, though she herself sensed no danger.

A moment after Momma spoke, however, Jake heard the muffled sound of cat paws thud to the pavement directly behind him.

He turned and saw a huge mountain of matted gray fur, gnarled and snarled like the bark of a crooked old tree. Big Gray had been hiding in one of the crates. Now he stood facing Jake with feet spread and head lowered like a bull about to attack. There was a look of madness in his yellow eyes as they rocked back and forth in their sockets. And a sinister smile played across his lips.

"So, you came to me, just as I thought you would." The smile turned into a grin and Big Gray's enormous teeth flashed in the dark alley.

Jake thought of making a run for it. But Big Gray was already too close. To run now would only force the big cat to attack. And there was something he wanted to say.

"Look here, Big Gray." Jake stood up tall on his hind legs. "Before you pounce or lunge or swipe at us, or whatever it is you intend to do, there's one question I want to ask."

"Just one?" said Big Gray with an air of coy amusement. "Why not two or three? Why not ten? For that matter, why not have a little quiz show right here in the alley? You can be the master of ceremonies! What a terrific stall that would be, my little friend!"

"Please, no more cat-and-mouse games," said Jake. "Just tell me *why* you've chosen to destroy my family, when it was *I* who made the mistake of biting you?"

"So you admit it was a mistake," said Big Gray, oozing malice from his wicked bloodshot eyes. "I accept your apology. But don't kid yourself. No lousy apology is going to save your miserable skin."

"I said I made a mistake. That's not the same as an apology," snapped Jake. "Now answer my question, you mangy maniac!"

"I forgot how yummy you look when you're angry," said Big Gray. "I shall miss our little talks when you're nothing more than a warm lump in my belly."

Jake was really worked up now.

"Skip the babble and answer my question!" he demanded. "Why can't you just take me and leave my family alone?"

"Very well. I'll indulge your *last* wish," Big Gray said with a self-contented sneer. "As it happens, the answer to your question is quite simple: It wouldn't be *enough* to kill you. I have to humiliate you the same way you humiliated me. It's pay-back time, pure and simple. The only way to even the score."

At this point Poppa called out, "Okay. I've heard enough of this mindless drivel! On the count of five we attack! Ready. *One . . . two—*"

"What, have you gone crazy?" Dexter whispered in Poppa's ear.

"It's just an old mouse trick," said Poppa under his breath. "*Three . . . four . . .* Instead of attacking on the count of five, we make a run for it . . . *FIVE!*"

Unfortunately Big Gray had been around long enough to know this particular mouse trick. On the count of five, instead of bracing himself for an attack he sprang at Jake.

It was a short leap and *almost* an easy catch. But Jake dodged Big Gray's outstretched claws. In a heartbeat he was off the pavement and into a crate of wilted lettuce.

"Nothing like a little salad with my meal!" Big Gray hissed and jumped into the crate.

As Jake burrowed to the bottom of the soggy lettuce, Big Gray dug down, flinging lettuce leaves left and right into the air. Soon the crate was empty and Jake was helplessly exposed.

"Look! A prize at the bottom of my box of Cracker Jack!" sneered the mean cat.

Big Gray reared up and with one swift pounce, pinned Jake beneath his paws. Then he put on a sad kitty face and pouted. "I'm *so* disappointed in you. That wasn't much of a chase, was it? I thought you could do better than that!"

Face pressed to the floor of the crate, Jake strained to lift his head and speak. "Want to back off and let me try again?"

"Nothing doing." Big Gray's pout melted into a malevolent leer. "Our little story has come to an end. And the moral is quite clear: *Mice who bite cats must die*!"

Big Gray's open mouth hovered above Jake like a black hole about to suck him into oblivion.

A drop of cat saliva fell onto Jake's nose and he struggled to wipe it away with his paw. "Eat me if you must," he said. "Just leave my family alone!"

Big Gray appeared insulted.

"I shall eat whomever I please, whenever it pleases me!" Suddenly Big Gray's nose twitched. "What *is* that most unappetizing odor I smell?"

"What smell?"

Big Gray sniffed again. "That smell! Eeew! It smells like . . ."

"Poison!" cried Dexter as he leaped into the crate with Big Gray and Jake. "Rat poison, to be exact!" Dexter winked in Jake's direction. "Smell me. I rubbed it on my fur too. Eat us and you die like a rat with its belly on fire!"

Jake immediately picked up on Dexter's intent.

"I told you not to tell him!" he said, pretending to be cross.

Big Gray's expression of smug victory abruptly shifted to baffled concern.

"Oh, this is good," he said, not really sure what to think. "This really is *excellent*!"

"Don't worry," said Dexter. "Even if he just mauls us to death he'll get enough poison on his paws to kill ten cats!"

"Really, you don't expect me to believe that? Do you?" asked Big Gray.

"Frankly no," said Dexter. "That's why I told you. When you're dying a slow poisonous death, I want you to know we were the ones that did it to you. You see it wasn't enough for Jake to bite you. I convinced him to *kill* you as well!"

"I don't believe you!" said Big Gray. "I don't believe a single word you've said!"

"Prove it," demanded Jake. "Kill me!"

"That's right! Kill us both!" said Dexter.

Big Gray sniffed again. When not prowling the streets, he lived a more than comfortable, pampered life in the home of an elderly lady. Never once had he gone down into the sewer, so its odor was completely unknown to him.

As Jake looked up into Big Gray's eyes he could see the gridlock of thought that lay behind them. A battle of fear and blood lust raged in Big Gray's mind. Jake and Dexter could only wait to see which one would emerge as victor.

"You're both liars!" Big Gray lifted first one paw and then another. "But I'm not taking any chances. Not for the likes of you two!" he snarled, and leaped out of the crate.

"Well, then." Jake stood up, shook himself and breathed a sigh of relief. "In that case, we'll be going too."

Big Gray was not listening. He had already turned to the puddle in the alley and was washing his paws.

Chapter 15

As soon as Poppa cried, "Five!" he and Momma and Baby Ben ran for their lives. Ducking under a wooden fence, they made their way through alleys and back streets until they reached the park. Then Poppa picked out a safe spot on a grassy hill where they would be sure to see Jake and Dexter's approach.

"We'll wait here," he said, and looked up at the morning sky still filled with the pink and yellow clouds of sunrise. "Pretty, isn't it," he said to Momma. "We really ought to get outside more often."

Momma quickly glanced at the sky, but didn't really *look* at it.

"Yes, it's very beautiful." She sighed. Momma's heart ached to talk about Jake but she didn't want to upset Baby Ben any more than he already was.

"Jake's dead," he sobbed. "I just know it! That mean ugly cat killed him. And someday he's going to kill us, too."

"Now, now," Momma's voice was both soothing and firm. "You don't know anything of the sort."

"Yes I do," cried Baby Ben. "Big Gray had Jake trapped in a crate. I saw it. There's no way he could be alive!"

"You have it all wrong," said Poppa. "There's no way that crude cat could eat my Jake. He's just not smart enough."

"I'm sure Poppa's right," said Momma. "Jake and Dexter will be here soon."

"We'll just wait for them. You'll see," said Poppa.

So they waited, and waited, until even Poppa looked discouraged and worried.

"Jake must have gotten lost," he said at last. "We'll have to meet up with him at the school."

"Does that mean we're going on without him?" asked Baby Ben.

"That's right," said Poppa sternly. "Now listen up. Going through the park means traveling out in the open through the grass. So stay together, and if anyone spots you, hide under a leaf."

The prospect of hiding under a leaf so thrilled Baby Ben his concern for Jake vanished almost completely. "That sounds like fun," he cried. "I want to hide under a *red* leaf."

"Stay close to me," said Momma, and the small family of mice set out across the grass, still wet with last night's dew.

Soon their fur was dripping wet. When Baby Ben sneezed, Momma expressed her concern.

"Don't worry, Momma," said Baby Ben. "It's just some pollen stuck up my nose."

Everything went smoothly until they reached the fountain in the center of the park. Baby Ben was having so much fun plowing through the wet grass, instead of following Momma and Poppa around the fountain, he continued on in a straight line.

"This is so great!" he cried. "It's like crashing through a jungle!"

"No, not that way, Benny!" called Momma.

Just then Baby Ben bumped into a park bench. The old woman sitting on the bench didn't see him. But her little dog, Doodles, did. All of a sudden Doodles jumped down and started barking in Baby Ben's face.

"This way!" called Momma.

Baby Ben had never seen a dog before, not even a little one. Of course, compared to him, Doodles wasn't little at all. He was enormous.

"Run!" cried Poppa.

But Baby Ben couldn't run. He was so petrified with fear he could hardly breathe.

Then Doodles spotted Momma and Poppa. Pretty soon the frantic little dog was running around in circles, jumping and barking wildly.

"Calm down, Doodles!" cried the dog's owner.

Doodles would not calm down.

The more the woman commanded, "Sit! Doodles, sit!" the louder Doodles barked. Pretty soon one of the park's many gardeners, armed with an arsenal of shovels, rakes, and cutting tools came over to investigate.

"This is not going well," said Poppa. Momma looked extremely worried.

All of a sudden Jake's head popped up out of the grass. Then Dexter's grinning face appeared.

"This way," they called.

Baby Ben was so glad to see his big brother he forgot to be afraid.

"Where are we going?" called Baby Ben.

"Just follow me," cried Jake.

"What took you so long?" said Poppa. "Your momma was getting worried."

"Tell the truth, Poppa," said Momma. "You were worried too."

"How did you get away from that monster?" asked Baby Ben.

"Dexter saved me," said Jake. "He was terrific! But I'll tell you all about it later. Right now we have to hurry. I think we stumbled onto a shortcut back to school."

"I'm all for shortcuts," said Poppa. "Lead the way."

"It's really more of a hitchhike than a shortcut," said Dexter.

"On the way here I remembered Molly telling me about this teacher, Miss Clark, who likes to get up early and watch birds in the park," explained Jake. "So when we entered the park I kept an eye peeled for her. And sure enough, there she was, sitting on a bench with a pair of binoculars."

Every once in a while Dexter or Jake poked their heads up out of the grass and looked around to get their bearings. They continued on in this manner for a few minutes until Dexter cried, "There she is, up ahead!"

Poppa, Momma, and Baby Ben stopped to look.

"What a nice lady," said Baby Ben. "I like her!"

"And look what's on the ground beside her," said Dexter.

"It looks like a book bag," said Momma.

"Quite a big one," said Poppa.

"That's right," said Jake. "With any luck we can hitch a ride in that book bag all the way back to school!"

Chapter 16

As Miss Clark pushed back the big white doors of P.S. 42 she saw Ava coming up the stairs.

"Guess what?" said Ava as she planted her feet squarely in front of Miss Clark.

Another teacher might have walked around Ava with nothing more than a quick "Good Morning." But Miss Clark stopped and looked down into Ava's big brown eyes.

"Now, let's see," guessed Miss Clark. "Did you lose a tooth?"

"No, I got all my new teeth. See!" Ava flashed a big broad smile. "But I'll give you a hint. It's about something *you* lost."

"Our new class pet?" guessed Miss Clark. "Have you seen it?"

"I did more than that. I held it."

Miss Clark could not have been more pleased.

"Oh, Ava, that's fantastic news! Where is he?"

"Down in Mr. Hobbs's workshop," said Ava. "You want me to come with you?"

"No, you run along to your classroom," said Miss Clark, and she turned toward the stairwell that led to the basement. "And thank you very much, Ava. You've made my day!"

"You're welcome," sang Ava, and she skipped down the hall.

"Did you hear that?" said Jake as Miss Clark descended the stairs. "They found you in Mr. Hobbs's workshop."

"That's funny," said Dexter. "I could have sworn I was right here in this book bag with you."

"We're in the school now, aren't we?" said Poppa.

"That's right," said Jake. "Welcome to your new home."

"I'll feel a lot more 'at home' when we get out of this book bag," Momma said.

"Me too," said Ben as he pushed aside Miss Clark's wallet and climbed over a pack of index cards. "It's squishy in here."

Mr. Hobbs, holding the lightbulb for the front hall in his hands, was locking his workshop door just as Miss Clark approached.

"Good morning, Mr. Hobbs," said Miss Clark cheerfully. "I believe you have our new class pet?"

"I think so," replied Mr. Hobbs. "At least, it's tame enough to be a class pet. Looks a lot like a mouse, though."

"Gerbils do look a lot like mice," said Miss Clark. "Can I see it?"

"Of course," said Mr. Hobbs as he fingered his large assortment of keys.

"I'm so relieved that you found our Dexter," said Miss Clark as Mr. Hobbs found the right key and placed it in the lock. "You have no idea how quickly children become attached to a pet. Even though he was only in the classroom for a few hours, I'm sure some of them were worried all night about how he was doing. They were thinking, Was he cold? Was he hungry? Was he safe?"

"I *was* cold and I *was* hungry and I *wasn't* safe!" squeaked Dexter.

"Shhhhhhh!" whispered Jake. "They'll hear you."

"I'm sure many of them included him in their prayers last night," Miss Clark said.

"I'm glad someone was saying prayers for me," whispered Dexter. "I sure needed them."

"It was very odd," Mr. Hobbs said as he pushed open the door to his workshop. "This morning when I came in, I thought I caught three mice. I flushed two of them down the toilet and was just about to dispose of the third when—"

As soon as Miss Clark saw Molly her spirits sank. She immediately rushed over to the aquarium and peered through the glass.

"You say you flushed two *mice* down the toilet?"

"That's right," Mr. Hobbs said. "This . . . this isn't your gerbil?"

"No," replied Miss Clark. "You were right the first time. It's a mouse."

"Gosh, I'm sorry," Mr. Hobbs said. "That means—"

"It's not your fault," said Miss Clark. "You didn't know."

Miss Clark sighed a deep sigh and reached—without looking—into her book bag for a tissue. Momma had to scramble to get out of the way when Miss Clark's hand came thrusting down into the bag. As Miss Clark fumbled around looking for her tissues

Jake quickly grabbed one and put it in her hand.

"Sometimes I think I get too involved with the children and their pets." Miss Clark blew her nose and threw the tissue back in the book bag.

"Yuck!" cried Dexter as the used tissue bounced off his head.

"I mean, I just love what I do. But I dread having to tell the children about something like this."

"I have an idea," said Mr. Hobbs. "Why don't you keep this mouse in your classroom for a while. It's very tame, you know."

"May the Great Mouse bless you, Mr. Hobbs!" squeaked Molly. "That's an excellent idea!"

Miss Clark looked into the aquarium again. This time, instead of looking glum, she smiled.

"She *is* cute," said Miss Clark.

"Very cute!" cried Molly. "Oh, please, please let me be your class pet!"

"You say she's tame?" Miss Clark asked.

"Very tame," squeaked Molly.

"Here, I'll show you," offered Mr. Hobbs.

When Mr. Hobbs lifted the screen and lowered his hand into the aquarium, Molly practically jumped into it.

"See." Mr. Hobbs lifted Molly out of the aquarium and scratched between her ears with an index finger. As he did so Molly leaned into his touch. "She likes that."

"My! She *is* tame," said Miss Clark as she extended her hand to take Molly. "Can I hold her?"

"Oh, yes! Yes! You can hold me!" cried Molly.

As soon as Miss Clark brought her hand close Molly stepped gently into her palm.

"It's hard to believe she's a wild house mouse," said Miss Clark. "But house mice carry diseases." And she quickly returned Molly to the aquarium and replaced the screen.

"Diseases!" Molly cried. "I don't have any diseases! I'm as healthy as an apple!"

"Are you sure?" Mr. Hobbs asked.

"It's a hard call," said Miss Clark. "Most of the kids would listen if I told them to leave her alone. But a few would have her out of this tank as soon as my back was turned."

"What if I cleaned her up?" asked Mr. Hobbs. "You know, gave her a bath or something?"

"May I?" Miss Clark pointed toward Mr. Hobbs's sink.

"Of course." Mr. Hobbs handed her a container of liquid soap.

Miss Clark squirted some of the soap in her hands and began to scrub them, which gave her time to think.

"I appreciate your offer," Miss Clark said as big globs of soapsuds fell from her hands into the sink. "But what if she bit one of the kids and they had to get shots? Or worse yet, what if they got sick and their parents sued the school? I might lose my job! And I love what I do too much to risk that. No, I'll just have to get the children a new gerbil."

"So what am I supposed to do with this mouse?" Mr. Hobbs asked.

"I guess that's up to you," said Miss Clark. "Luckily you don't have the same responsibilities I do. If I were you, I'd consider keeping her as a pet."

Chapter 17

As soon as Miss Clark entered the classroom she was surrounded by a group of jumping, hand waving, shouting kids.

"We heard Mr. Hobbs found Dexter," James Peterson cried.

"Is it true? Is it true?" demanded Samantha Morgan.

"No, I'm afraid it's not true," said Miss Clark with a sigh. "Well, yes . . . actually . . ." Miss Clark pushed through the knot of children that surrounded her at the door, hung up her jacket, and set her book bag down next to her chair. "Take your seats and I'll explain to everyone what I think happened to Dexter."

The kids never got in their seats so quickly. Even those involved in completely different matters were soon dragged to their desks and told to be quiet by other students. In a matter of seconds the room was completely drained of kid noises and conversation. And all eyes were trained on Miss Clark.

"Well, I'm afraid Dexter is no longer with us," began Miss Clark.

"We know," said Martin. "He got loose yesterday!"

"Yeah, we want to know what happened to him," said Samantha. "Did Mr. Hobbs find him or not?"

"That's what I'm trying to tell you," said Miss Clark. "Mr. Hobbs did find him. . . ."

Suddenly the classroom broke out into an explosion of cheering, foot stomping, hooting, hollering, and spontaneous applause.

Miss Clark, wearing a somber expression, raised her hands to quiet the class and continued. "Mr. Hobbs found our Dexter in one of his mousetraps."

After a stunned moment or two of silence, Janie Smith raised her hand.

"You mean Dexter is dead?"

Miss Clark cleared her throat.

"I'm afraid so."

As soon as those words were spoken, a hushed "Ohhhhhh!" spread through the class.

Immediately Laurie Mars and Sandra Foster started crying. Big tears welled up in Laurie's eyes and fell like raindrops onto her desk. And Sandra just sniffled in a way that was hard to distinguish from her sinus condition.

"Did it hurt?" Tommy Benson asked.

"That's a dumb question," said Martin. "Of course it hurt. Those traps can snap a gerbil's back like a toothpick."

"I imagine it did hurt, Tommy," Miss Clark said, ignoring Martin's comment. "But I'm sure it was over very quickly."

"You bet it was," said Martin, and he slapped his hands together loudly. "Like that!"

"Oh!" Nancy Thomas shuddered. "That's gross!"

"What happened to the body?" asked Oliver Snarch, whose father owned and operated Snarch Funeral Home.

"I'm afraid Dexter was flushed down the toilet," Miss Clark said.

"Like poopie!" giggled Joey Cosgrove, who was usually one of Miss Clark's quietest students, except in matters related to bathroom humor. Then he often laughed the longest and loudest.

"That's not funny," said Laurie as she wiped her desk dry with her sleeve. "That's not funny at all!"

"No body, no funeral," said Oliver. "It's that simple."

"We can always remember Dexter," said Sandra, still sniffling. "He was the cutest little hamster I ever saw."

"Gerbil," corrected Miss Clark. "Dexter was a gerbil."

"That's right," said Sandra. "He was the cutest little gerbil there ever was. He had cute little ears and cute little eyes . . . I just wanted to hold him and hold him all day long."

Dexter heard all of this from inside Miss Clark's book bag.

"Gosh, I'm starting to miss myself," said the much flattered gerbil as he crawled to the top of the bag.

"Are you thinking about going back?" asked Momma.

"How did you know?" asked Dexter.

"You'd be a fool not to," said Poppa. "Free room and board and no danger. You can't beat a deal like that."

"Well, to tell you the truth, I have been thinking about it," said Dexter. "But it's not the easy life that appeals to me. I'd pick freedom over that any day. It's what I want to do with my freedom that counts. You see, I never had much of a real family back at Pretty Pets, but I'm starting to think maybe I could have one here, in the classroom with the kids. Besides, Jake's right. I *belong* in a cage. Out here I *am* a danger to myself and everyone I'm around."

"You certainly weren't a danger to me back in that crate with Big Gray," said Jake.

"Thanks," said Dexter. "But I know I still have a lot to learn."

"I have an idea," said Poppa. "Why don't you stay in your cage and be a class pet in the day time. And spend your night times with us. That way you can have *two* families!"

"That's a great idea, Poppa," squeaked Baby Ben.

"Shhhh, not so loud," said Momma.

"But how would I get out of my cage?" asked Dexter.

"That's easy. We'd just let you out," said Jake. "Cages are easy to open from the outside."

"Okay then," said Dexter. "My mind's made up. I'm going to give this class pet thing another try. And take night classes at survival school!"

"I'd say you've made a wise choice," said Poppa.

"Very wise," said Momma.

As he climbed over the rim of the book bag, Dexter stopped and turned to Jake.

"Wait a minute. What about Molly? You think she's all right? I mean, maybe I should stick around and help you guys rescue her?"

"Knowing Molly, I'd say she doesn't need any rescuing right now," replied Jake.

"Well, in that case . . ." Dexter stretched forward and gave Jake a nose touch. "I'll see you later."

"When it gets dark out," said Jake.

It was an easy jump from the book bag to the floor. Then Dexter marched up one of the aisles toward Miss Clark.

No one noticed Dexter until he reached the front of the classroom and hopped onto Miss Clark's foot.

"What?" Miss Clark jumped. Then she looked down and squealed. "Look, everyone! It's Dexter! He's back!"

Chapter 18

As soon as Miss Clark had left his workshop, Mr. Hobbs closed his door and sat down in front of Molly's aquarium.

"So what am I supposed to do with you now?" he sighed. "I'd like to keep you as a pet. I really would. But I get paid to exterminate mice. Not to raise them. You may be cute, but you're still a pest, vermin of the worst sort! And it's my job to rid this school of you and your kind."

"Hey, wait a minute," Molly said. "You're not actually thinking of . . ."

Mr. Hobbs stood up and opened the furnace door.

I can't believe this is happening, thought Molly. *One moment he cuddles me like a baby and the next he's ready to incinerate me! What kind of a world is this, anyway?*

Mr. Hobbs reached over to his desk, took a tissue from the box and blew his nose. Then he threw the tissue in the furnace and closed the door.

"So what am I going to do with you?" Mr. Hobbs continued.

"I guess you could just take me for a ride and drop me off someplace," Molly said.

"I guess I could just take you for a ride and drop you off someplace," said Mr. Hobbs. "But where? Unless I take you to the other side of town, you're bound to come back. Then I'll end up killing you in one of my traps one day. If I'm going to do that, I might as well kill you right now."

Mr. Hobbs opened the furnace door again. This time Molly felt the heat from the flames come right through the glass and warm her face.

"No, please!" cried Molly. "Not the furnace. I promise. I won't come back. Really. I promise!"

"But I don't want to kill you," Mr. Hobbs said. "And if I take you for a really long ride somewhere miles from here . . . chances are, you wouldn't last a day in foreign territory, what with winter coming on."

Mr. Hobbs lifted the mousetrap from his workbench and threw it in the furnace. Then he closed the furnace door and sat down with his face so close to the aquarium glass it fogged over with his breath.

"Golly!" Molly said. "I can't believe you just did that!"

"So what am I going to do with you?" said Mr. Hobbs.

"I guess you could just let me go," Molly said.

"I guess I could just let you go," said Mr. Hobbs. "As long as you don't fill this place with all your relatives, no one's going to mind a few mice around."

"My relatives!" said Molly. "Heck, no! All my relatives live in a deli. There's no reason any of them would ever want to move in here!"

"So I guess that settles it." Mr. Hobbs reached out, picked up Molly's aquarium, and set it down on his floor.

"You're just going to let me go?" Molly said.

"I'm just going to let you go," said Mr. Hobbs as he took the screen off and turned the aquarium over on its side.

"Now you get out of my sight before I change my mind!" said Mr. Hobbs. Suddenly Mr. Hobbs remembered the day he had to part with his dog, Captain, and his eyes began to moisten. "And don't you tell anyone I did this," he said with a quiver in his voice.

Molly knew she had to leave, but she didn't want to go without saying good-bye. As soon as she climbed out of the aquarium she ran over to Mr. Hobbs's hand and nuzzled it with her nose.

"Yeah, I'll miss you too," said Mr. Hobbs. And he let Molly rest her face against the soft part of his hand for a long time. Then he picked up the aquarium and said, "Now scoot!"

Chapter 19

Molly left Mr. Hobbs's workshop by the front door. Then she walked slowly over to the loose brick and disappeared into the wall. So much had happened in so short a time, Molly felt numb. One thing she knew for sure, she was going to miss Jake horribly. Slowly making her way through the wall toward the nest site, she couldn't help thinking about him. Just knowing that his empty nest would be waiting for her, filled her with a sadness as huge as she was small.

Then Molly turned a corner and smelled Jake's fresh scent. *Could it be he's still alive?* she wondered. *Or is my nose playing tricks on me?*

Molly raced the rest of the way to the nests. What greeted her there was the happiest sight she had ever seen.

Momma and Poppa and Jake were seated around Molly's homemade table, chewing on some macaroni and beans from Jake's knothole pantry.

"Just in time for breakfast!" said Jake.

"Oh, Jake!" cried Molly. "How did you ever survive?"

"You don't think I'd let a little thing like being flushed down the toilet ruin my day?" Jake said with a grin.

"Of course not!" Molly said, smiling.

She greeted her momma and poppa with hugs and kisses.

It was the warmest of greetings. For a long, long time Momma and Poppa held Molly so close she couldn't tell her own heartbeat from theirs.

Baby Ben, on the other paw, refused to be hugged.

"None of that mushy stuff for me," he said. "I've had enough lately to last a lifetime!"

"Sorry," said Molly with a smile. "I'm just so glad to see you. That's all."

"And we're overjoyed to see you!" said Momma. "You and Jake were always our favorites."

"Oh, Momma," giggled Molly. "You say that to all your children!"

"Only because it's true," said Momma with a wry smile.

"Soon as we rest up a bit we'll start building ourselves some nests," said Poppa.

"That's right," said Momma. "A house is not a home without a nest."

"I like looking out this hole," said Baby Ben as he peered through the peephole at Miss Clark's class. "What's going on out there?"

"Oh, Benny! There's all kinds of great things happening out there," Molly said.

"That's right," said Momma. "We're in a school now. So you're going to get an education."

"I don't want an education," said Benny. "I want to have *fun!*"

"Education is fun," said Poppa. "You'll see."

"Oh, I almost forgot!" cried Molly. "How's Dexter? Did he make it too?"

"Sure did," said Jake. "But now he's back in his cage."

"He was captured?" asked Molly.

"Oh, no," Jake said. "He went back on his own."

"Good for him," Molly said. "I think he'll make a great class pet."

"Maybe so," said Jake. "But he still wants to stay enrolled in our survival school."

"*Our* survival school?" said Molly. "I like the sound of that. I like it a lot!"

Just then Momma called Molly to her side. "Come, sit down and have something to eat," she said. "We have so much catching up to do, so much to talk about."

"I *want* to talk," said Molly. "But I'm not hungry. Mr. Hobbs just gave me some cheese."

"Mr. Hobbs *gave* you cheese?" gasped Jake. "I don't believe it."

"Fed me right from his hands!" boasted Molly.

"This I've got to hear more about!" Jake cried.

"It's a long story," said Molly, and she stopped to peer out the peephole. Three kids had just taken Dexter out of his cage. One held him. One offered him a peanut. And one gently stroked his back. "It's a long, long story. And it's not over yet!"

About the Author

Frank Asch has written and illustrated nearly sixty children's books, including picture books, poetry books, and novels. He is perhaps best known as the creator of the Moonbear series. He performs puppet shows for children in his hometown of Middletown Springs, Vermont.

Don't miss the other exciting adventures in the Class Pet series, *The Ghost of P.S. 42* and *Battle in a Bottle.*